Fenella

A Fable of a Fairy Afraid to Fly

Written by
Susannah Cord

Illustrated by
Ditte K. Gade

Brown Books Publishing Group
Dallas, Texas

Debts of Gratitude

This book would not have been possible without the support and encouragement of friends and family. Thank you to Ditte Gade aka Deedee for finding Fenella in the line of her pencil and the sweep of her paintbrush. To my father Jes C. Boye-Moeller for finding Deedee—and for the neverending supply of support and enthusiasm and faith in Fenella. Thank you to Grith, mother of Zoe (and Sander, min Sveskel), dear friend who always, always, says just the right thing, at just the right time. Special thanks to my brother Christian for marrying the right girl, and for bringing me back to earth when necessary, in such a gentle and encouraging manner. Last but most definitely not least, my love and gratitude to the best and most supportive—in every way!—husband a girl could ask for. Well, they could ask, but he's already taken. Lucky me.

Fenella: A Fable of a Fairy Afraid to Fly
©2010 Susannah Cord

Written by Susannah Cord
Illustrated by Ditte K. Gade

Manufactured in the United States of America

For information, please contact:

Brown Books Publishing Group
16200 North Dallas Parkway, Suite 170
Dallas, Texas 75248
www.brownbooks.com
(972) 381-0009

A New Era in Publishing™

ISBN-13: 978-1-934812-80-8
ISBN-10: 1-934812-80-3
LCCN: 2010935411

www.FenellaTheFairy.com

CPSIA facility code: BP 304168

For Zoe

There once was a beautiful land far, far away—beyond mountains and valleys, blue skies, night skies, thunder, lightning, and shooting stars. It was a land of emerald green hills, deep and lush forests full of chattering birds, and meadows of wildflowers that bloomed all year. Tinkling streams flowed into raging rivers that poured over tall cliffs into roaring waterfalls that ended in cool, clear pools of crystal water. It was a peaceful, magical land, and in this land lived a fairy named Fenella.

Fenella was a fairy like most fairies in most ways. So teeny-tiny she could slip right through the eye of a darning needle, Fenella had lots and lots of golden hair that curled all the way down her back. Her eyes seemed to fill up a great deal of her face, and were the color of those clear pools that the waterfalls fell into—green and silver or blue, depending on the weather. Her skin had the sheen of pearls and glowed with the magic that flows through fairies' veins. Her laughter was music that moved flowers to release their perfume, and when she sang even the nightingale paused to listen. She had the voice of a thousand silver bells stirred by a gentle summer breeze. Fenella was a fairy who would make any fairy mother proud.

Except for one thing. There was one thing that set Fenella apart from all other fairies that ever lived, and it was a horribly bewildering and confusing thing. It went against everything anybody ever heard of fairies. It went against the very nature of being a fairy, and it was the cause of great concern to all who knew and loved her. Most of all, it was the cause of much pain and embarrassment to Fenella herself. The flowers no longer trembled to her laughter and the nightingale sang by himself, for Fenella neither laughed nor sang these days.

Fenella was afraid to fly.

She had long since passed the age when fairies first take flight, but she had yet to so much as float from a blade of grass to the ground. It wasn't for lack of trying. Every morning at sunup, Fenella watched as her family and friends flew off. They swung their bright and colorful wings faster and faster till they were just a blur, soaring gracefully into the sky, dipping and diving and gliding, making it look as if it were the easiest thing in the world, which it was. At least, to them it was. To Fenella, it seemed like the most impossible thing in the universe.

But every day, when Fenella was sure they were all gone, she stepped out into the clearing, determined that today would be the day she flew—the day that her wings exploded into color.

Today would be the day her wings changed from the milky white of a fairychild too young to fly to the colorful wings of a fairy dancing on the wind. Today she would receive her new name to match her new wings.

And she would try. Oh, how she tried.

She flapped her wings. She flapped them faster. And faster. Her wings fluttered through pale shades of blue and green and purple; they shook and they trembled. She stood on her tippy-tippy toes, her arms reached for the sky and her legs lengthened, ready to take flight. She jumped a few times in case her wings would believe they were flying and truly carry her. Fenella closed her eyes and clenched her jaw, trying to imagine how fun it would be, how good it would feel to leave the solid ground beneath her and fly through the air. She tried to imagine the happy smiles of family and friends, the relief on their faces when they saw her take wing.

But all Fenella could feel was the terror of nothingness surrounding her, the thin air and her feebly flapping wings that she would not trust to support her. All she could see was the disappointment on her mother and father's faces when they came home to see her, pale and grounded as always. All she could think about were the whispers that followed her wherever she went, asking why she, Fenella, only child of Midnight and Summer, was still colorless and walking when she should be flying in brilliant color. The whispers said she was an embarrassment to her father, Midnight, so named for his deep blue and silver wings, and to her mother, with her beauty, her grace, and the leafy green and gold wings that had made her famous throughout the land. And yet, with all their fame and beauty and grace, their only child was a disaster.

This particular day was no different. There she was, trying with all her might to let go while all the time her mind held her fast. It was as if the earth itself grabbed hold of her ankles and held her down. Exhausted, Fenella gave up and flopped in the grass, picking at the blades and throwing them at an invisible enemy, her face all pinched up and tears pricking at her eyes.

"I'm a fairy," she muttered under her breath. "I'm a fairy, I'm a fairy, I'm a *fairy,* and I *must* fly!"

She thumped the earth with her fists.

"I'm a fairy, I'm a fairy, I'm a fairy, and I *will* fly!" she yelled at the top of her voice, scaring a ladybug into flight.

"Of course you will, Twinkles," said a deep voice behind her, "and I think I know how!"

It was her father, Midnight, and he sounded excited. He wouldn't tell her what his idea was, only that he just knew it would work and that he was a fool for not having thought of it before.

"Climb on my back, Fenella," he said. "Fold your wings up tight now, honey, you and I are going for a little ride and then, we are going to see you fly!"

Fenella climbed on, feeling ridiculous and babyish. With her arms around his neck and her eyes shut tight, they took off into the air. Midnight's strong wings beat steadily and Fenella felt safe, as long as she didn't think about all the empty space around them. She tried to think what this great idea could be, to feel excited that she could possibly be flying in no time at all, but the very thought that she may soon be flying on her own terrified her. So instead she imagined the sound her beating wings would make as she flew. She pictured the colors by which she would be known and admired, the colors that would give her a new and wonderfully grown-up name.

Fenella dreamed of flying through the air, her wings no longer wishy-washy and ugly, but swirling colors of blue and green and purple, red and yellow, or silver and gold. No one had ever seen such wings, and in their surprise and envy of her beauty, they would all forget who she had been. She would no longer be the only fairy ever afraid to fly. Fenella would be the fairy with the most magical wings. She would be free to roam wherever she pleased, alone or with friends, free to come and go, free to dance and soar and glide on summer wind—no more walking ever again.

With a light bump, Midnight and Fenella landed on a large, bright yellow daisy. Fenella opened her eyes, unfolded her wings and sighed. Her wings were as pale as ever, almost see-through and still drooping.

To her relief, her mother was there. She felt somehow safer with her there, too. Summer was looking at Fenella closely.

"How was practice this morning, Fenella?" she asked, her lovely green and gold wings flickering with hope.

"Oh," said Fenella and slumped down beside her mother. "The usual." She hung her head and fiddled with a lock of hair.

"Well your father has had a splendid idea, and we think you are going to be flying in no time at all, Twinkles. Did you tell her yet?" her mother asked her father, who stood beaming down at them both, obviously enormously pleased with himself and his splendid idea.

"Fenella," he said, folding his wings to sit down in front of her. He took both her hands in his. "It will happen. You *will* fly. Your wings will light up with your color or even several colors, and before you know it, you'll be racing through the air with the rest of us, wondering how you could ever have been afraid to fly. It is the most natural thing in the world for a fairy to fly and . . . ."

"Midnight," her mother sent her father a warning look, "just tell her."

"Well, anyway, Fenella," he continued, pulling gently on one of her curls and watching as it bounced back, "I think that you just need to jump into it and let your natural instincts as a fairy take over. It is that simple. You just jump into it!"

"Jump into it?" Fenella hoped he wasn't saying what she thought he was saying.

"Yes! Jump!" He beamed even more. "Just walk out onto that petal, take a deep breath and jump! You'll see. Your wings will take it from there. Besides, your mother and I are both here in case . . . well, I have no doubt this will work." He looked uncomfortable and said no more, just smiled what was meant to be a reassuring smile.

Fenella's stomach curled and clenched and knotted. She hardly dared to look at them, afraid she would burst into tears. How could they possibly think she could walk out there and *jump*?

"You can't be serious," she said. "Please tell me you're not serious. I'm afraid of heights, you know that. I can't go out there. I can't. I *can't!*"

"Just try it. Please, Fenella." Her mother's voice cut through her fear. She thought of how embarrassed they must feel, to have a daughter like her.

Fenella got up, and, holding on tightly to her father's hands, she began to back out onto a petal.

"Don't let go, Papa, promise! Not until I'm ready." Fenella kept her eyes on his chin, her own chin trembling, her hands shaking. She felt clammy and cold all over, her stomach was churning, her legs were wobbly and weak.

It seemed like it took years, but finally she was standing at the very tip of the petal, her legs shaking uncontrollably under her. The daisy shook with her. Fenella peeked over her shoulder. Her wings hung limp and gray, and the ground looked like it was a million miles away.

Fenella stood there for a long time, her heart thumping in her chest. Finally she took a deep breath, willing herself to let go, to let herself fall into space, to trust her wings to unfold and carry her. She saw the ground rushing up at her, she felt her wings spread and then . . . nothing. She might as well not have wings, as little as they responded to her.

"I can't, Papa," she said, a big, blue tear rolling down her cheek. "I'm so sorry. I just can't. I know I am a big disappointment to you and you probably wish you'd never had me and, and . . ." The rest of Fenella's words disappeared in a sob that was followed by another, and another, and then she was back on the daisy, safe in her mother's arms, crying with shame.

"There, there, Fenella. Don't be foolish," her mother mumbled into her hair, holding her close. "You'll fly. It will be alright. Don't you ever think we would rather be without you; you could never disappoint us. We just want you to be happy, and as long as you won't fly, you won't be happy, and then we can't be either, see?"

For a long time they sat there, Fenella, her mother, and her father. They told her things they had never told her before. Her parents told her that she was all they ever wanted and for the longest time they had longed for her. In all those years of marriage without a child, she was what they dreamed of and she was the most precious thing in the world to them.

After a while it didn't seem so bad after all that she wasn't flying—yet. Fenella started to think that maybe one day she might be able to fly after all. If her parents could love her and believe in her still, after what just happened, then she could, too.

"Now," said her mother, "you just rest here a little while, and we'll be back soon. I think maybe you could use a little time on your own now, fairychild. The breeze will rock your daisy and the sun will soothe you, and the birds will sing you to sleep. Dream of all things good and kind and beautiful. We won't be far, and when you wake, you will feel ever so much better." With that, and a kiss from them both, they flew off into the afternoon sun.

Fenella watched them float away, playfully zigging and zagging through the wildflowers. Their wings flashed brilliantly in the sunlight. She pulled up her legs and rested her head on her knees. Her pale wings grew paler and drooped like wilting flowers. Now that they had left, she felt alone and miserable. She no longer felt as if she might fly some day. She just felt like one big failure. The tears began to flow again, puddling around her in a soppy yellow mess.

"Excuse me! Excuse me!" sang a breathless little voice right over Fenella's head. "Excuse me! Oh, I say, if you would be so kind, move over just a tad, I could come down for a sip—such a juicy looking daisy. Excuse me!" Fenella looked up to see a gaily colored butterfly flitting from side to side over her head.

"Oh, certainly," muttered Fenella and scooted over. She hoped the butterfly wouldn't notice her red eyes and the soppy daisy.

24

"I am Mademoiselle Butterfly, pleased to make your acquaintance, how do you do," whispered the butterfly, her wings flicking slowly as she extended a long straw right into a mess of tears and yellow pollen. "Oh dear, hm, oh dear, I say, oh *dear*!" she exclaimed, her wings now flapping in alarm. "I say, there is something *dreadfully* wrong with this daisy!" She made a funny rattling noise as she pulled her straw free and smacked her lips in distaste.

"I'm sorry, it's all my fault," mumbled Fenella, hardly daring to look at Mademoiselle Butterfly.

Mademoiselle Butterfly held still for an unusually long moment as she looked right at Fenella for the first time.

"Oh!" she said, gasping a little. "Surely not. You? A pretty little thing like you?"

"Yes, me!" cried Fenella. "I was crying because I'm afraid to fly and I'm much too old to be such a baby, but my wings are just as pale and useless as a toddler's and I upset everybody and I'm their only child and I'm . . . I'm . . . I'm . . ." Fenella didn't know what else she was, and besides she almost choked on her outburst, so she stopped talking and started hiccuping instead.

"Oh! Oh! I say!" Mademoiselle Butterfly opened and closed her wings twice in surprise. "But flying, my dear, is as natural as breathing to we winged creatures, surely you realize?"

"I dooo—*hic*—oo!" wailed Fenella. "It just isn't to meee—*hic*—ee!!"

"Aha! I see! I see!" replied the butterfly, although she clearly did not see at all. "Well, I must say. A fairy afraid to fly. Well, well. I never heard of such a thing. Rather silly, really, but if you say so, I suppose you're right. You are a fairy after all. But afraid to fly? How peculiar. How odd. Yes, yes, very odd indeed." She prepared to fly off, her antennas feeling for the winds around her, her wings ready for take-off.

"But wait!" cried Fenella. "How did you learn to fly?"

Mademoiselle Butterfly paused a few inches away, then flew from side to side with quick jerks of her wings.

"Learn to fly, dear? How awful!" she sang out in her whispery voice. "How perfectly ghastly! I didn't learn to fly—I simply flew! See?" She flicked from flower to flower, further and further away. "I just let the wind carry me, dear, I just chitchat with the wind and we dance along. Simple, dear, simple . . ." The last Fenella heard was the butterfly's whispery laughter as she sang "*Learn to fly? Whoever heard of such a thing?*"

"Well, thanks a bunch," mumbled Fenella, hugging her knees to her chest. "Thanks a whole bunch."

Fenella was daydreaming, imagining her wings dancing with the wind when a loud buzzing noise interrupted her daydream.

"Mizz! Mizz, oh, bzz, bzz, phooey, no time for dallying, bzz! Bzz, Mizz?" The buzz and the fast-talking voice came from behind her. Fenella turned around to see a bright yellow and black striped bee, impatiently zipping a little from side to side, peering at her with beady little black eyes.

"Yes, sir?" said Fenella politely.

"Bzz, in a hurry, no time, to dilly-dally, bzz, if you'd move over, bzz, I could dip in, bzz, be on my, bzz, way, in no time, no bother, no fuzz, no muzz, *bzz*!"

"Oh," Fenella blushed, then explained, horribly embarrassed to be causing everyone such trouble. "Well, the thing is, you see, well, this flower is ruined. I mean, I ruined it. It doesn't taste good anymore, Mademoiselle Butterfly just said so herself. I was crying, you see, because I, well, I am afraid to fly, and now the daisy is all salty and yucky. I'm so sorry."

While Fenella was explaining, the bee was scooting from side to side, looking at Fenella with one eye, then the other, cocking his head, buzzing impatiently.

"Ruined, you zzay, eh? Zzalty? Bzz, no good, no, no good for the Queen, no, no, must be zzweet, bzz, too bad, bzz, such a juicy flower, too, bzz, zzzilly twit , aren't you, ruining a perfectly good daizzy, bzz, afraid to fly, you zzay? Whoever heard of a bzz, fairy afraid to, bzz, fly?"

"I know!" said Fenella, her face scrunching up as she tried not to cry again. "I know it's silly, I don't even know why I'm so afraid. I try, really I do, but . . ."

"*Bzz!* Nonzzensе!" interrupted the bee, eager to be on his way, "Bzz, nothing to be afraid of. You, just fly. That's, bzz, what God gave us, wings for, bzz, and thank goodness, too. Who'd want to, bzz, walk? Walk? Bzz! Phooey!"

With a quick nod of his head, he turned to fly away.

"But wait!" cried Fenella. "Please, sir, Mr. Bee, before you go, I know you're awfully busy, but please, tell me, how did you learn to fly?"

"Bzz!" shouted the bee as he flew a quick circle around the daisy before lowering himself down so he was face-to-face with Fenella, his wings flapping furiously. "I say! Bzz! Buzzy is right, young lady!" he said sternly. "On Her Majesty's buzzinezz is what I am. Bzz! Her Majesty's Business, no lezz. The Queen commands, bzz, and I obey. Yezz, that'zz the way of it. Bzz. Buzzy, buzzy, obeying the Queen. Learn to fly? Bzz! How ridiculous! Bzz! As silly as a fairy afraid to fly! As uzzelezz as a bee with no Queen to pleazze! Ha! Bzz! Who has time to learn to fly? Bzz! Not I, not I! No, no—out the hive, off we fly! No time, no time, bzz, to *learn* to fly, bzz, it's fly or die! Fly or die!"

And off flew the bee, buzzing loudly as he went, so all would know he was on serious business for Her Majesty the Queen.

"Fly or die? Phooey yourself!" muttered Fenella. "Well then I may as well lay down and die, for all I'm worth."

And so Fenella lay down, feeling helped not at all by the bee or the butterfly. She lay in the daisy, swaying gently from side to side in the breeze, all curled up with her head on her arms. The sun warmed her skin and she no longer felt like crying. She was tired and drowsy and empty. Soon Fenella was somewhere between sleep and waking, a pleasantly calm and quiet place in her mind where her thoughts drifted lazily like leaves on a slow river.

Everything and nothing in particular flowed through her mind, and for once, it wasn't all about her fear of flying. She thought of all the things her parents had said to her this afternoon. She thought of the love they had shown her today, and a little smile curved her lips when she realized that she was not an embarrassment to them, that she never had been. They thought she was beautiful and clever. They thought she was the best thing that had ever happened to them. They had no doubt she would fly one day, and even if she never did, they only cared that she was happy. Fenella sighed and fell into a deep, restful sleep.

The daisy shook and quivered. Fenella woke, her eyes swollen and scratchy from crying. She wanted to stand up to see what all the shaking was about, but just then the daisy swung violently from side to side, see-sawing madly, and Fenella was thrown down on her back, feet in the air. She rolled out over the side and would have fallen to the ground if the daisy didn't stop jiggling just then. Instead she lay very, very still on a petal, holding on tightly as she tried to catch her breath and understand what had happened. Very carefully she looked down.

Fenella's stomach leaped into her throat. She was high above the ground, higher than she had ever been. Not only that, the daisy seemed to be flying! The wind sang softly through the petals and the wildflowers below her looked like toy flowers because they were so far away and dwarfed by the distance. All around her was nothing but empty air.

With a low whimpering sound in her throat, Fenella clambered back to the safety of the daisy's center. Breathing hard, trying not to think of how far away the ground was, Fenella looked up instead—right into a pair of enormous brown eyes, peering down at her. Fenella had never seen such big eyes—they were large enough for her to swim in. Her heart raced, her mind struggled to understand what she was seeing.

"People!" she whispered, remembering the stories she had grown up with. She had heard stories of people who were big as trees, with heavy hands and hard hearts, who had forgotten about the fairyfolk and the magic that lived in their midst. "People!" she whispered again, certain that her life was over. "But I can't die now—I never learned to fly! If only I could just fly away, they'd never catch me. *If only I could fly!*"

"What's that, Mommy?" The eyes looked up and Fenella saw another face, even bigger, looking down at her. It blocked out the sky as it looked at Fenella.

"That's a bug, honey, just a little bug, but we don't want to take the bug home, just the flower. The bug lives out here in the meadow."

A bug? thought Fenella. *A bug? I'm not a bug! I'm a fairy, can't she see that? I'm no bug! Bugs are silly creatures, they would just sit here and let you take them home, they wouldn't even know where they were,* raged Fenella at the woman. *You don't know where you are,* said a spiteful voice in her mind. *You're not flying off, are you? You're just sitting here, letting them take you wherever they want. You're no better than a bug.*

"A bug! Eek!" shrieked the little girl and held the daisy as far away from her as she could. Fenella saw a glimpse of blue sky over her head.

I am no bug, so don't shriek at me, thought Fenella indignantly.

Could have fooled me, answered that spiteful voice in her mind.

I am not a bug just because I just can't fly, retorted Fenella, now very angry at both the child and the mean voice coming from somewhere inside her. She was standing up now, fists on her hips, glaring at the child.

Just because you won't *fly,* corrected the voice. *There's a difference between* can't *and* won't, *you know. You can fly, but you* won't.

Because I'm afraid, cried Fenella, torn between anger and hurt at being betrayed by something inside herself. *I try and I try, but I just can't let go!*

Fly or die, said the voice, now very quiet and calm. *Fly or die.*

"What do you mean?" cried Fenella, feeling very alarmed.

But the voice was silent.

"Honey," said the mother now, "Just blow on the bug and it will fly away. Go on, deep breath."

Fly away? thought Fenella, watching in terror as the child's cheeks filled up with air into huge balloons about to be emptied onto her. *Fly away? But I can't fly, I mean I won't, I mean, oh, I don't know what I mean, I just don't fly, I . . .*

And that was as far as Fenella got in her befuddled mind. A great whirlwind came blowing over her, and she was turned over and over till she held on to just the tip of a petal, clung to it with all her might, thinking of the long fall to the ground. *Fly or die,* buzzed Mr.Bee. *Fly or die,* sang Mademoiselle Butterfly. "Fly or die," whispered Fenella as the petal slipped out of her hands. Fenella tumbled helter-skelter through the air, her wings crumpled and useless against the wind. Over and over she somersaulted on the current of the child's breath until finally it weakened and she was free falling towards the earth, it was rushing up at her, faster and faster. "Mooommmy!" screamed Fenella, and with the force of that scream, her mind cleared, her heart leapt, and her fear gave way. Her wings unfolded with a snap and burst into color.

With a quick one-two of her wings, Fenella had righted herself before she knew what she had done. A gentle breeze blew and lifted her even further from the ground, her wings fluttering gently as she balanced herself easily and let the wind carry her. A funny feeling rippled through her, like cool water running over your skin on a hot summer day. Fenella tipped her right wing into a steep curve and spun around so fast she almost fell to the ground after all. But with another *whoosh* of her wings, Fenella brought herself to an absolute standstill in mid air, her wings beating rapidly and smoothly. Then she let herself drift on the breeze again while she caught her breath.

It wasn't long before Fenella began testing her newfound skills. She became more and more daring. She did somersaults, backflips, nosedives, twists, and spins. She flew far and fast, low and slow. She raced the hummingbirds and she slalomed through the forest, dodging trees and teasing the slow ladybugs. She laughed till she thought she would burst with the joy of flying and the freedom therein. Back in the meadow she flew from flower to flower as she had seen the butterflies do, and let her hands stroke the silky petals as she floated by. She sang and she laughed, and the meadow became thick with the scent of wildflowers and loud with birdsong. It wasn't long before it became loud with the chatter of fairies, too, but Fenella heard not a thing, she was so wrapped up in flying, until the voice of her mother called her.

"Fenella! Fenella! You're flying, and oh! Look at you. Look at your wings! The colors. Have you ever seen such *colors*? And so many! Midnight! Midnight! Come see, come see! Fenella is flying and look at her wings!"

Fenella woke as if from a daze. Stopping in midair, she looked around to see herself surrounded by fairies, gaping at her in amazement. There was her mother and father, tears of delight and pride streaming down their faces.

"Look, Mother, look, Papa," was all she could think to say. "I'm flying!"

"Yes, we know, Fenella." Her father was laughing at her.

"But your wings, Fenella," said her mother, unable to say anything else, so choked by emotion was she.

"Yes, Mother, they're working!" said Fenella proudly and did a little pirouette in the air.

"We know they're working, Twinkletoes," said her father, "but have you had a look at them?"

"My wings . . ." Fenella clapped a hand to her mouth. Her wings! In all the excitement of flying, she had forgotten all about their new color. Fenella took a deep breath and turned her head ever so slowly, partly excited, partly afraid of what she would see. Would they be blue? Green? Red? Would they be pretty? She hardly dared to look, afraid she would be disappointed after all the joy of the afternoon.

They were a starburst of color, a rainbow come to life in her wings. Fenella had never seen the like of them. No fairy ever had so many colors in their wings. Fenella's wings were every color she had ever dreamed of—blue, green, red, yellow, purple, gold, silver. Colors she had never known existed. They flowed and trickled and roared like the streams and rivers and waterfalls. They flickered like the wildflower meadow in a breeze.

She turned around and around herself, staring and staring and staring at what she had become. She was beautiful, she was graceful, and she flew like the wind. She glowed like a rainbow in the sun after a spring rain.

"Fenella, you look like a rainbow!" exclaimed her mother.

"A dancing rainbow!" said a voice in the crowd.

"A rainbow dancing!" cried her father.

"Rainbow Dancer!" went up all the voices of the fairyfolk.

"Rainbow Dancer," whispered Fenella.

Fenella had her winged name. From now on and for all eternity she would be known as Rainbow Dancer, the fairy with the rainbow that came to life in her wings. Soon no one would remember the little pale fairy who was so afraid to fly. Now they just nodded wisely and said so many colors and such beauty take their time to unfold—all in due course, all in their own good time. Fenella the Rainbow Dancer danced with the wind, her fear lost in time.

. . . and for Mom, who always believed I could fly